James Kinghorn
9 Rathgar Ave.
Ealing, London W13 9PL

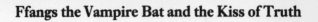

Ffangs the Vampire Bat and the Kiss of Truth

ff

Ffangs
The Vampire Bat
and the
Kiss of Truth

Ted Hughes

Illustrated by
Chris Riddell

faber and faber

LONDON · BOSTON

First published in 1986
by Faber and Faber Limited
3 Queen Square London WC1N 3AU
This paperback edition first published in 1990

Photoset by Parker Typesetting Service Leicester
Printed in Great Britain by
Cox and Wyman Ltd Reading Berkshire

British Library Cataloguing in Publication Data

Hughes, Ted
Ffangs the vampire bat and the kiss of truth.
I. Title
823'.914[J]   PZ7
ISBN 0-571-15461-1

Contents

Chapter One

Trials of Attila

I

All the chickens grew up to be hens.
All but one. Attila!
All the hens were laying their eggs.
But not one egg from Attila!

Attila shook his rooster tail and crowed:
Cockarockarooooo!
Attila's face was bright as a bugle as he crowed:
Cockarockarooooooooo!

'We don't need that,' said the Farmer.
'We'll cook him and eat him!'
He came with a carver.

'Kill me? Cook me? Eat me?' cried Attila.

He fled. He fluttered. He flew, he flew.
Out of the farm and over the field
And into the wild wood: Whoooosh!

'Free!' he gasped, 'I'm free! I'm – Aaaarghle!'

A fox had grabbed him by the neck.
A greedy fox, with a grin full of grippers
Clamped tight on Attila.
So the fox spoke with his eyes. And his eyes said:
'I've gotcha! I've gotcha! Now I'm going to eatcha!'

3

'Oh no!' cried Attila. 'Oh no! Let me go!
I'll call all my hens, the white and the black.
You can eat all my hens. The dappled and the grey.
As for the red ones, you can eat them in threes.
You'll be eating hens for a week, I tell you.
Just let me live to the end of the thirteenth hen.'

The fox's greedy eyeballs bulged.
But he'd hardly opened his mouth to say,
'Call them here quick –', and Attila was away.

'I'm free, I'm free!' cried Attila.
And he flew high out of the wood.
And he saw the clouds like palaces.

But 'Bang!' said the sky. And 'Bang!' And 'Bang!'

'Bang, bang, bang!' said the earth.

Feathers were floating.
Pheasants were falling. Dead, and dead.
Pheasants to left of him. Pheasants to right of him.

Attila's fright was a sight, his comb went white.
Suddenly he forgot the art of flight
And he fell on a gunner's head.

'Catch him and eat him!' was the cry.
Attila looked round, and every eye
Was saying: 'We've got you. Now we're going to eat you.'

4

The Cook thought he was dead as a duck.
Attila heard the knives going Skerwhickety-whack!
He ran from the kitchen looking backwards
Straight into the clutch of a gypsy.
The gypsy took him home in a sack.
'Cook him quick, let's eat him,' cried the Granny.

'Oh no,' said the gypsy.
'He's worth more as a parrot Up For Sale.
With that shivering, shimmery fountain of tail
He'll make a lovely parrot.
I'll clip his wings, so he can't escape.
Then all he'll need is a bent beak.'

So the gypsy clipped his wings
And bent his beak, like a parrot's.

The gypsy took him to sell at a fair:
'Buy this Parrot – a glorious talker!
He'll sing the National Anthem!'

Attila was bought by a long-nosed Fool.
He pecked the Fool's nose, and he ran.

He flapped the flappers the gypsy had clipped
And he ran and he ran and he ran and he tripped
Down a black hole.

5

Bump he fell on his rump among beer-barrels.
It was the cellar of a Pub called 'The Cock'.

A brewer's man was rolling barrels down into the cellar.
He found Attila and carried him up to the landlord.
'We must have knocked your sign off,' he said,
'I'm sorry. And it got its nose bent.'

The landlord was overjoyed.
'A sign from Heaven!' was what he cried.
'He looks like a fighter, with his broken nose.
I've always wanted to start up some cock-fighting.
It's good for trade.
He'll be the challenger. He'll take on all comers.'

Attila blinked his eyes, and thought: 'What's this?'

6

Attila was the Champ!
He fought every fighting cock that came.
Flurried them, floored them, and defeated them all.
He grew famous. What a fighter!
The crowds guzzled Ale and goggled at Attila.
The Landlord grew rich
With all the prizes he won with his bent-beaked champ.
He re-named his Tavern 'The Bent-Beaked Cock'
And called Attila 'The Bent-Beaked Bomber'.

Attila became so famous
A thieving hand grabbed him by the legs as he slept

And stuffed him into a black bag
And a voice hissed:

    'For Falcons, race-horses and fighting cocks
     The oil-Sheikhs pay in solid, pure gold blocks.'

Stop thief! Stop thief!
Too late.

And Attila cried: 'After all this
Do I end up a Kebab?'

7

A police-car wailed. The thieves' van skidded in the rain and
crashed into a tree. And the black bag shot out through the
smashed windscreen.
Attila was free and he ran.

He ran through the land. He ran. He ran. And the day
passed.
And the days passed. And he ran.
Every morning he crowed:
He beat his growing wings and he shouted: Cockarockaroo!

And listened for an answer.
No cock shouted back. No cockarockaroo came back. No
cocks crowed.
Not one cock! And Attila thought:
There are plenty of pretty houses here
But no cocks and hens. Only broilers.

And he crowed a lonely Cockarockarooo!

'Where is the happy land of cocks and hens?
Where is the happy land of cocks and hens?'

So Attila came to the sea.

A ship was setting out. Attila flew up into the top of the mast
and he crowed:

'Take me away to the land of cocks and hens!'
But the Captain cried: 'Catch that stowaway cock!'

The Ship's Cook crawled up to catch Attila,
With his cleaver between his teeth.
And as he crawled closer and closer his eyes grew larger
And larger and larger. And his eyes were saying:
'We've gotcha! We've gotcha! Now we're going to eatcha!'

8

Attila flew to the bow. He flew to the stern.
The whole crew joined in the hunt.
The Cook cried: 'Slice the onions!'
At that very moment
The ship hit a reef.
The crew cried Help! And the ship went down.
And where there had been sailors, now there were shark-fins.

Where's Attila, the castaway cock?
There he is, dripping and shivering,
Perched on top of an empty floating egg-box.
But he's not alone.

All the sharks rear up to show him their tonsils
And all their little pebble eyes are saying:

'We've gotcha! We've gotcha! Now we're going to eatcha!'

9

Suddenly the sea opens, and up comes a whale.
Its eyes like screw-holes, its mouth like an aircraft hangar
And Attila is on the long black slide
Into the whale's belly.

In the belly of the whale Attila heard a shout.
Robinson Crusoe stood in the door of his hut
Built on the whale's liver. 'Ahoy there!
Welcome!' cried Crusoe, 'Just what I need!
A beautiful alarm-clock!'

And so when dawn shone down the whale's throat
Attila crowed in the echoing belly of the whale:
'Cockarockaroooooo!
Where is the happy land of cocks and hens?'
And Crusoe got up to catch a mackerel for breakfast.

'This is the life,' said Crusoe, 'Sing it again.'
And Attila sang:
'Where is the happy land of cocks and hens?'
But after that he moped, with one eye closed.

And Crusoe had to sing for himself:
    'There is a happy land
    Far, far away!'

Suddenly the whale was caught in a whirlpool.
Then the whirlpool reared up, on its tail,
In the middle of the sea. And the whirlpool swayed,
The whirlpool became a waltzing waterspout.
The waterspout did a big dance over the sea
Leaning and twirling
And the whale whirled in its coils, with corks and bottles,
High up over the sea.

And all in a whirl Attila spun out of the whale.
He spun away over the sea,
Spinning in the waterspout
With whale and corks and bottles,
Spinning over islands of crabs and islands of monkeys,
Spinning more and more slowly

Till the waterspout was weary
And Attila fell at the end of the world
On the island of ghosts.

23

The ghosts crowded aghast, to gawp at Attila.
Attila stared at all the ghosts, astounded.

They were a shock of shivering and queer shapes.
But they all cried: 'A god has fallen!'
(They were simple ghosts.)
'This is a god,' they cried, 'fallen from Heaven!
In all his flying gear! Look at his colours!
Be our King, O god, be our King!'

The simple ghosts did not know what a cock was.
But Attila knew a ghost when he saw one
And his every feather stood up on end.

Then he remembered: Ghosts are afraid of Cock-crow.

So he crowed at the ghosts: Cockarockarooooooooo!
It worked.
The ghosts scattered in the blast, they scattered like mist,
They twirled away under the ground, into worm-holes.

Attila was more astounded than ever.

The ghosts came creeping out, fingers in their ears.
'O do not crow at us with your deadly crow.
Be our King.
Lead us against our enemies.
Your terrible trumpet will shatter our enemies.'

'It's quite true,' said Attila, 'I'm a fighter.
But who are your enemies? Are they ghosts, like you?'

'Our enemies,' said the ghosts, 'are the vampires.'

'The vampires?' cried Attila.

'The vampires!' cried the ghosts.
'Lead us against the vampires!'

The ghosts' fleet of ghostly ships sails out
Crammed with ghosts
And Attila sails in the flagship.

And the vampires are waiting.

The Island of Vampires is black with vampires.
The trees of that island are hung with vampires.
Their eyes are like the lights of a city seen from the night sea,
And the eyes gleam on the fangs
Waiting for the army of ghosts.

Attila had his secret weapon.
He flies up into the air
And he dives down on to the black mass of the vampires
Shouting COCKAROCKAROOOOOOOOOOOOOO!

No vampire can stand a cock-crow.
The vampires set up a howl like a million wolves.
They sweep up into the air
Like a black cloth snatched off a table
And they vanish into an old volcano
Like washing-up water going down a plug-hole.

Attila cried: 'The battle's won'
And looked round for the ghosts.
But they'd heard the cock-crow too
And they'd vanished too. They just couldn't help it –
Gone like a gasp in their fright at the crowing of a cock!
And their ships bobbed empty.

Attila strolled along the sands of Vampire Island.
He met a lonely vampire.
'What's this?' snarled Attila fiercely. 'Why aren't you with all
   the others

Inside the volcano?
Didn't you hear my irresistible cock-crow?'

'Yes, I heard,' said the vampire.
'But I'm not really a vampire.
I can't stand the sight of blood, let alone the taste of it.
I'm a failed vampire.
I don't want to be a vampire.
I want to get back to the world and become human.'

'Alas!' said Attila. 'I see you nearly are human.
But here you are, human on Vampire Island
Far from the happy land of human beings!
And here am I, a cock on Vampire Island,
Far from the happy land of cocks and hens.
What can we do?'

'Climb on to my shoulders,' said the vampire.

And he flew, did that vampire.
Attila gripped the fur of his neck
Till they came to Jungle-Fowl Island.
'Here you are,' said the vampire. 'Here's your land.
This is the Happy Land of cocks and hens.'

'This is the place for me,' cried Attila.
'But what about you?'

The vampire had taken off again, alone.
He flew out over the surf.
Like a flag torn off a mast, he blew out over the sea.

'My story's only just started,' he called,

And he flew towards the land of men.

Chapter Two
Ffangs Flees Forwards

I

Ffangs the vampire landed in London.
Lonely he roamed the streets before dawn.
'I don't want to be a vampire,' he sang.
'I don't want to drink blood.
I don't want to sleep all day in a grave.
I'm sick of being a hideous vampire.

I want to be human and happy.
O how do I do it? Where do I start?'

2

He met a thief bowed under a bag of loot,
Creeping home in the grey of the dawn.
'Good morning, sir,' he said politely.
The thief dropped his bag, his eyes ballooned.
His hair spiked up in stiff prickles.
He yelled:
'No! No! No! It can't be! But it is!'
Ffangs blinked his blood-red eyes.
'I'm a friendly!' he cried, 'I'm a harmless non-vampire.'
But the moment he opened his mouth
His fangs flashed and clashed

And the thief streaked with a shriek, then squeaked: 'Police!
O help! O Police!'

41

3

Ffangs gave himself up.
He walked into the Police-Station.
The night-shift policemen gasped and went white.
A vampire looks like a vampire.
Ffangs began to explain:
'I'm a vampire and it's driving me crazy – '

What had he said?
The cops had all become birds.
They were swooping out through the windows.
They had become squawking and hurtling geese
When a fox bursts into the goose-house.

Ffangs, too, let out a doleful cry:
'Why am I so horrible?'

43

4

Ffangs had a brainwave.
'I'll give my story to the newspapers.
I'll tell them "A Vampire's Inside Story"
And how I don't want to be one any more.
And how I want to be human.
Then everybody will know I'm harmless and good.
And they will let me live like a person.'

He flapped into the Editor's office.
The Editor gave one gurgle, then bolted.
Ffangs flapped behind him, shouting: 'I'm a vampire,
I've got a great story for your paper.'

The newsmen stampeded from their desks.
The secretaries fainted like mown grass.

Ffangs clashed his fangs:
'Why won't the idiots listen to me?' he raged.
'Why can't they see I'm a trusty?'

45

Ffangs wept. He tramped down Oxford Street
Wearing sandwich boards with foot-high letters:
'I am a harmless vampire, help me to be human.'

The side-streets were jammed with fleeing tourists.
The great stores barricaded their doors.
They did not like his drooling fangs – oh no!
They did not like his blood-red eyes – oh no!
Or his trailing wings black as plastic.

The whole centre of the city let out a screech
As Ffangs ran up and down crying: 'I'm safe'.

Some went cross-eyed with fright.
Those who fainted were lucky.
Dogs had fits and every roof
Was hopping and hissing with pop-eyed cats.

48

Ffangs thinks: Best to go straight to the Boss.
He flies to the Houses of Parliament.
The Security Guards shout: 'That was some pigeon!'

Ffangs flies into the Council Chamber.
All the Ministers lie there heaped on their benches
Like the wounded on a battlefield.

'Which is the Prime Minister?' cries Ffangs.

The Prime Minister is quick-witted.
Already, nothing is left of him but his empty shoes and a few
    floating flakes of dandruff.

Then all the MPs
Hurtle towards exits – cartwheeling,
Somersaulting, vaulting, or simply whizzing through the air
    like darts.
A flock of their papers flutters out after them.
And Ffangs cries: 'Imbeciles! I'm good!
Tell England I only want to be English and human.'

He sits sobbing, alone, in the Speaker's Chair.

Already every TV in the country carries the stop-press news:
'Rabid Vampire Empties Parliament.'

7

Ffangs tries again: 'The Queen will help me.
Nothing scares Queens.'
He soars to Buckingham Palace –
But news had got there before him, the Guards stood alert.

A blast of bullets met Ffangs.
But plain bullets can't hurt a vampire.
'I'm a vampire,' he cried, 'but I'm friendly.'

Then a blast of anti-tank shells hit him.
But they can't hurt a vampire. He came on,
Crying: 'I only want to be human!'

Missiles blazed clean through him, but they can't hurt him.
He just gets up again out of the smoke.
'I'm tired of blood,' he wails. 'Let me be human!
Let me in to talk to the Queen –' Then Boooomp!

A tiny nuclear bomb plants a reeking crater
Just where he'd been standing.
But there he is, flapping in the air, like a big black ragged
    butterfly,
Crying: 'Listen to me! Are you all deaf?'

Then the garrison flees. A helicopter
Hoists the Queen away. Ffangs roams
Alone and lonely through the empty corridors of the Palace
Gazing sadly at all the glittering gems.

8

A helicopter has landed.
The Vampire-Hunter has arrived – Squarg
Straight from Transylvania.
Belts of silver bullets, fatal to vampires.
A repeating rifle, a fearless beard, and a dreadful tread.
He stared like a bear. He boomed like an echoing cave.

Ffangs watches him on the Queen's TV and trembles.
And he sees a film of himself – little red eyes
Peering from the Palace windows,
And he hears: 'Her Majesty has escaped. But
Where will the vampire strike next?'

And he heard Squarg, the grizzly Vampire-Hunter,
Demanding a pretty girl. Squarg boomed:
'A pretty girl, with rosy lips and rosy cheeks
And plump as a sausage. Bait for the Vampire.
So he can drink her blood.
Then he'll drop in a drunken sleep.
And when he's asleep I'll get him. This is how it's done.

So bring me a pretty girl. The prettier the girl
The drunker he'll get on her blood
And the deader I'll kill him.'

Crafty Squarg! He knew Ffangs could hear him.
Crafty Squarg! He kept his plan to himself.
He's not going to wait for the vampire
To drink himself into a doze.
He's going to shoot on sight.
He's going to kill him dead with his tongue hanging out.
But he keeps this to himself.

All England reels with shock. What?

Give one of our loveliest lovely lovelies
To that bloodsucking monster? Squarg is mad!

9

But Ffangs has a brainwave too! A plan!

At night as England turns
Under the moon in fearful sleep
Ffangs launches himself from the Palace roof, like a big
   beetle.
He peeps into bedrooms.
At last he finds what he's looking for –
That year's Beauty Queen: Sweety Crisp!

He slips into her dream. And he whispers
'Offer yourself up to the vampire.
I am an angel. I will protect you from him.
You will save England from the vampire.
You will be so famous the Queen will wash your feet,
And sugar models of you
Will be sold to China by the ton.
You will be a TV series all to yourself:
"Sweety Crisp And The Vampire".'

And to make the dream real he stuck a five-pound note
Between her sleeping fingers
Whispering: 'You have been chosen.'

Then he flashed back to the Palace
And Sweety Crisp awoke with wide eyes and a cry:
'I'm going to offer myself up to the vampire!'

Then her mother fainted and her father
Went as white as a plate, and said: 'What next!'

10

The Queen gave Sweety Crisp a bravery medal.
And here is Sweety
Already front-page news, and a big picture of her
Pretty as a flower
Shaking Squarg's giant, black-haired, horny, vampire-killing
    hand.

Everything is prepared. In the main hall of the Palace
Sweety stretches her famous body out on a divan
And seems to sleep, looking as luscious as she can.

But what's this now? An interruption!
Squarg's plan is rolling into action.
A giant strawberry has arrived at the Palace, on a lorry.
It wears a huge label: 'Present for the Queen
From British Homegrown Inc.' Nobody knows
Crafty Squarg is crouching inside it
Hugging his vampire-gun.
Ten men carry The Strawberry into the Palace
And leave it. Through two tiny holes
Squarg fixes his eyes on Sweety Crisp.
She does not know he's there, nor does Ffangs.
Squarg smiles in the dark. He's done this before.
Ffangs will be his three hundred and twenty-first vampire.

Ffangs has a simple little plan.
Ffangs will explain to Sweety Crisp
That he's harmless, and only wants to be human –
He'll simply hold her hand.
Then the whole country will see that he's harmless.
They'll sip some of the Queen's best port together
And Sweety will say: 'You know, you're quite cute.'
So he'll prove to the world he's no vampire
But a good chap.
Sweety Crisp might even stroke him, for all to see – and envy.
That's his little plan.

But as he enters the hall, flitting sootily, like a chimney moth,
He sees that giant, scarlet Strawberry!

Greed! Greed! Vampire greed!
For the juice of a Strawberry! He can't resist it!

He plunges his fangs deep, deep O deeper
Into the Strawberry
And deep into Squarg.
Squarg cannot believe it! He bellows,
Bursts like a bomb from the Strawberry
And flees.

12

Now the Police, the Army, and Squarg
Advance against the Palace.
All of them have silver bullets in their guns.

Squarg is furious. His plan has misfired.
Everybody is furious.
TV commentators are nodding their heads on puppet threads
    at each other.
'The Vampire' they are saying, 'is probably
Drinking Sweety Crisp like a bottle of Pepsi-Cola
Inside the Palace, this very moment.
What disgusting scene
Are the people of this country going to be forced to look at
    next?
It's outrageous.
Squarg should be sacked.'

But there is Sweety Crisp, on the Palace steps,
There on the crimson carpet,
There in all her prize-winning beauty –

Sweety Crisp! Leading Ffangs by the claws!

Sweety Crisp on television
Introduces Ffangs to the Queen. And she strokes him.
There he is, black-furred and red-eyed, having trouble with
    his wings, being polite.

13

The Queen commands the Lord Mayor of London
To set up Ffangs
In a Restaurant.
'We sincerely hope', she says, 'that this will encourage
All our vampires to cut back on blood.'

Ffangs feeds his customers
With oozing steaks and livers and stuffed hearts,
And with whatever they want in that line.

But out in the kitchen he buries his furry muzzle
In strawberries and cream. Then more
Strawberries and cream. Then more. And more
Strawberries and cream.
And sometimes, for a change, cream and raspberries.

14

Now hear what happened to Squarg.
He married Sweety Crisp. What a wedding!
It was all fixed up by television.
So you can guess how fantastic it was. It was fantastic!
Ffangs was Squarg's best man.
Sweety Crisp became Mrs Thomas Squarg.
And the Queen gave them a present: a pair of solid silver
    pistols.

Then into Tom Squarg's helicopter – and home for their
    honeymoon
To his vampire-hunting lodge
High in the beautiful mountains of Transylvania.

His hunting lodge was a tower.
Little did beardily-smiling Thomas
Or Sweety Crisp with her laughter of dazzling teeth
Little did they think,
As the helicopter landed on top of the tower,
That their troubles had only just started.

15

They danced together down into Squarg Towers.
There was the feast waiting.
There was the sumptuous four-poster bed
And there was the elegant table.
Caviare! A salmon! Chocolate mousse!

Thomas slapped his brow. 'No!' he cried.
He'd forgotten the Champagne!

'I'll get it in a flash, my love,' he called. He leaned from the
    stair and kissed her.

'Unpack your suitcase. I'll be back in a blink.'
He leapt up the stair.

As she hauled out her Beauty Queen wardrobe
His helicopter rose from the tower.

He didn't see the big dark wings clinging under the parapet.
He didn't see the Vampire Bat, its talons buried in the
    stonework.
A great bag of black fur, hanging on the wall of the tower
With its red eyes staring up. And he flew off.

And he didn't look back
So he didn't see it squeezing into the tower
Through a window,
Dragging its wings after it.

Chapter Three
The Rat Wife

I

Thomas Squarg was back, with the Champagne.

He landed on top of his tower.

He came down his spiral stair, calling his wife: 'I'm home. I'm home.'

No answer.

He put down the crate of Champagne.

He sniffed the air, hoping to smell rich perfumes. He went from room to room.

Where was his wife?

He went into the bedroom, thinking she might be feeling a little weary with travel.

He saw a small bump under the smooth coverlet.

He whipped off the coverlet.

And his eyes popped.

2

What crouched there was a rat.

A rat. In his bed!

'Out!' he roared. 'Out, rat!'

But the rat only cowered shivering. He peered at it more
   closely. Was it a sick rat?

Then he heard its thin voice.

'Help me, O help me!'

Thomas frowned. That was a woman's voice. Very tiny and
   thin. Was it his wife?

He couldn't believe his ears.

He picked up the rat and gazed into its eyes. Had his wife
   become a rat?

Impossible!

This is a trick, he thought. My enemies the vampires have
   stolen my wife, and left in her place this trick rat. A talking
   rat!

At that moment, the tower began to shake.

3

Chairs waddled across the room.

Was it an earthquake?

He clasped the rat in one hand, fell to his knees, crawled to
the window and looked out.

Deep canyons surrounded his tower,

But now his tower was rising swiftly away from them. He saw
the mountains dwindling away below.

What was happening? Was his tower flying on its own into the
clouds?

Then he looked up, and shouted aloud with amazement and
anger at what he saw.

And the rat which he still clasped, and which was or was not a
woman, and was or was not his wife, squealed with fright.

4

A giant hand held the top of the tower in its finger and thumb.
The tower was being lifted.
Then the foggy cloud swirled at the windows, and he could
see nothing.
Then brilliant sun dazzled his eyes. He was above the clouds!
Then Bump! the tower was set down. Thomas ran up to the
top of the tower. He was furious.
But when he got up there and gazed round – for the first time
in his fearless career he was speechless.

5

Gigantic faces, each as big as a good-sized church front,
surrounded him, and gazed at him with solemn eyes.
He heard thunder. But the thunder was words. It was a voice.

'We want you to help us,' said the words.

There were nine faces, large bushy faces. His tower stood on a giant hand, that held him up near the faces.

'Help us,' rumbled the thunder. 'Help us against the Giant Vampire.'

He saw one of the mouths move. Behind the giant heads he could see stars. Was he out in space?

The rat, which was or was not his wife, had fainted. He still clasped the warm little body.

'How can I help?' he shouted.

Thomas was not easily scared.

6

Suddenly the thunder banged louder than ever. He saw all the faces twisted wildly upwards.

'Here it comes again!'

And he saw the jagged wing of a giant vampire above, blotting out some stars, before the huge hand which held the tower closed over him, and Thomas toppled back down the spiral staircase, still clutching the warm rat.

7

What was happening? He had no idea.
He clung to the bottom post of his stair in the dark, while the tower swung and rocked and jolted, as if it were being carried by somebody running.
The little rat had come to, and in the dim light he could see big tears rolling out of its eyes. Can rats cry real tears?
'Who are you?' he asked. 'If you're not a rat?'
But as the rat began to speak the tower came to a stop, and an eerie blue light filled the rooms.

8

Once again, Thomas ran to the top of his tower. This time he was more surprised than ever.

A giant, black, furry face stared at him, even bigger than the faces before. Enormous red eyes.

Expert as he was, he knew a vampire bat when he saw one. But what a bat! Above its head he saw great planets, as big as suns, with their moons spinning around them.

His tower was held in giant, glossy black claws.
All around he saw the bare crags and gorges of a strange
   planet.
This must be the King of all vampires. The god of vampires!
He had to admit it, he felt helpless.
He clasped his trembling rat.

Then he heard a rushing, fluttering wind. It was a voice. It
was words.

'Help me,' said the words.

The Vampire Bat was actually asking him for help. Thomas
looked into the eye-pupils. They were like cathedral
doorways when the inside of the cathedral is lit at night.

'We know what a champion you are, we vampire bats. Only
you can help us,' said the voice.

But then the dreadful, black, furry face twisted round and let
out a thin cry. 'Here it comes again! We're too late!'

Thomas now felt ready for anything. It was just as well.

Bounding towards them, leaping through space, leaping from
planet to planet, closer and closer,

Was a gigantic rat!

Inside Thomas' shirt, where he had put her for safety, the
little rat began to screech and screech.

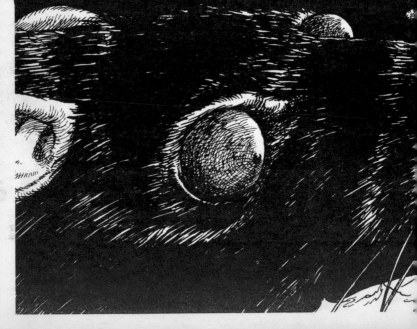

Once again he toppled back down his spiral stair, this time on
purpose, to escape the rat.

And once again the tower was rocking. The tower was
turning upside down. The tower was spinning. The tower
was falling through space.

The Vampire Bat must have dropped him and fled to save
itself.

He clung again to the stair-post, and was wondering where
you land when you fall into space, when the tower stopped
with a bumpety jolt and a crashing. The little warm body in
his shirt was whimpering.

11

He crawled to the nearest window and peered out.

His tower had lodged in the branches of an immense oak tree. Each leaf was the size of a double bed. The acorns were as big as fat children.

He saw something moving. The huge rat's face peered down between the branches. It was still coming after him.

Then the giant rat spoke.

12

'Give me my wife,' is what the rat said.

Thomas looked up at the round black eyes. The rat was smaller now than it had been. Even as he watched, it grew smaller.

The rat in his shirt suddenly squealed: 'Ataturk!'

Thomas understood. He lifted her out.

She leaped from his hands into the oak tree, crying 'Ataturk!
    Oh Ataturk!'
The big rat, now no bigger than a cat and shrinking rapidly,
    stood on its hind legs to greet her. The two rats embraced,
    sobbing loudly.

Then Thomas called up through the leaves: 'OK, you've got
    your wife back, but where's mine?'
The rat that had been huge, but that was now only rat-size,
    the planet-rat, came towards him, and jumped in through
    the window. As far as looks went, it was now just an
    ordinary rat.

13

The rat led Thomas down towards the cellars of his tower.

But the cellars no longer existed. The cellar stair led down into empty space, and broke off.

Far below, Thomas could see the trunk of the oak tree, growing up from a grassy field.

His tower was lodged in the branches of the tree.

The rat leaped from the bottom step down on to the wrinkled bark of the oak. Thomas followed.

He gripped his pistol with its vampire-killing silver bullets in his right hand.

The rat led into a hole in the oak tree. Thomas followed.

Inside, a spiral stair led down. It reminded Thomas of his tower.

The rat turned and spoke: 'This is the stronghold of the King of the Vampires. He stole your wife, to avenge himself on you. He stole my wife, and put her in your bed, to make you think your wife had been turned into a rat.'

'So where is Sweety Crisp?' cried Thomas. 'What did he do with her?'

The rat pushed open a door. 'There she is,' he said.

14

Thomas blinked.

The room was blindingly bright. It was like looking into the reflector in a lighthouse, millions of candlepower.

Then he made out, on a bed, a tiny figure, the size of a rat. A tiny woman asleep.

Amazed, he picked her up, and she woke.

It was his wife. 'Sweety!' he gasped. 'It's impossible!'

She burst into tears.

'Now,' said the rat, 'you have found your wife.'

'But what's happened to her?' cried Thomas. 'How do I get her back to the right size?'

'Maybe it's you who are too big,' said the rat, and it leaped away up the stair of the oak tree, and vanished.

Thomas sat there on the bed, and looked round at the
festoons of diamond and ruby and emerald rings, hanging
from the ceiling like strings of tiny dazzling onions, and
clasped his sobbing wife.
Was she too small, or was he too big? One of them was going
to have to change.

At that moment a shadow crossed the room, as if the blinding
light of the jewels had failed for the fraction of a second.
Then he heard a familiar sound.

15

What he heard was the whiffle of a giant vampire's wings.
He pushed his wife down his shirt front, where he had kept
the rat, and sat there, pistol in hand.
Would this be the strange Vampire that had asked for his help
on that strange planet? Had it followed him?

Then came that same rushing, fluttering wind, and he heard the Vampire speaking:

'I asked you to help me,' it said.

It must be clinging upside down out there, thought Thomas, with its claws hooked into the rough oak tree bark.

He raised his pistol. Then he shouted: 'Why did you take my wife?'

There was a silence. Then the Vampire said:

'She is not your wife.'

Thomas frowned.

'What do you mean, she is not my wife? My wife is my wife. Sweety Squarg, née Crisp. I know my wife. And now I've got her back, even if you have shrunk her a bit.'

But the Vampire answered:

'Before she was your wife, she was mine. My wife. She was a beautiful vampire. Yes. The rats changed her into a woman and you married her, O Fool!'

Thomas frowned, so that it seemed his eyes might splinter. He took the tiny woman out of his shirt. She had heard everything.

'Well, is it true?' he asked her. He didn't know what to think.

Then, to his absolute horror, she nodded.

Chapter Four
The Little Snake

A scuffling clattering sound came down the oak tree stair.
The Bat's giant face, upside down, filled the bottom of the
stairway. Its red eyes blinked as Thomas levelled his pistol.

'She's my wife,' said Thomas. 'And I'm going to keep her.'

The Vampire's red tongue flicked over its snout, and it
blinked.

'Give me my wife,' it said.

'She's mine!' roared Thomas, and his brow went dark red.

'You heard what she said. Ask her again,' said the Bat.

'Don't you dare move,' said Thomas, and he kept his pistol
aimed at the Bat's chin. Then he spoke to his tiny wife,
holding her quite lightly in his left hand.

'Are you his wife or mine?' he asked.

She did not answer. She put her hands to her face and
covered her eyes. Thomas asked her again. He even gave
her a slight shake.

'Whose wife are you, his or mine?'

Then Sweety Crisp began to sob again. She couldn't speak. She couldn't answer. She sobbed.

Thomas didn't know what to do. He felt terrible. If he killed the Vampire Bat, with a silver bullet, what then? She might scream: 'You've killed my husband!'

But then the Bat spoke.

'There is only one way,' it said. 'Let's go back to the beginning. Before she married you. Before she married me. Let's start again.'

'How can that be?' cried Thomas. 'What's happened has happened. We can't undo it. We can't go back and start again.'

'Oh yes we can,' said the upside-down Bat, and again his red tongue flickered over his snout.

'There is a person,' said the Bat, 'who can make time go backwards. Find that person. If you find that person, everything can be changed from the beginning. Everything will happen differently. All our mistakes will be corrected. And who knows, it might turn out then that she really will be your wife. Or it might not.'

Thomas lowered the pistol. What was the Bat saying? How could time be made to go backwards? How could anything go back to the beginning and start afresh? Those were crazy words. He felt his head spinning.

Suddenly he felt the little woman in his hand become hard. She had become a doll. He examined her, mystified. She had become a hard shiny doll, with bright, silly doll's eyes, and big eyelashes, and a shiny, red mouth.

'Put her down where you found her,' said the Bat. 'Now that she's a doll she can wait. Dolls don't get bored. Now go. Search for that person. I promise, I shall not steal her. Here you see me as a vampire bat. This is a mistake I made. I have searched and searched but I cannot find that person, to make time go backward, and to undo my mistake. I am not brave enough. But you can find that person, maybe. Correct my mistakes. Help me.'

Thomas gazed at the Bat. Here it was again, asking him to help it, just as it did up among the planets.

'Where do I begin?' asked Thomas. 'Where do I start looking for this magic person?'

'Follow me,' said the Bat.

2

The Bat made himself small, no bigger than a bee. He flew and Thomas followed. They came to a town.

'Whoever I land on,' squeaked the Bat, 'might be the one we're looking for. Keep your eye on me. I'm looking for a corrected person, one whose mistakes have been wiped clean. He will know how to direct us.'

Nobody noticed the Bat, dodging along the crowded street, going round and round over heads, dipping low and veering up again. Till Thomas, who never took his eyes off the dithering black dot, saw it land on a man's shoulder, light as a ball of soot.

A smart, brisk man, with silver-rimmed spectacles and a glittering watch. He was just stepping into a bank. He certainly looked as if he'd finally got things right.

'Excuse me, sir,' called Thomas. 'Can you help me?'

The man's eyes went wide, and he felt his wallet bulge under his jacket. Thomas the Vampire-Killer had trimmed his hair, and shaved his beard, but his black moustache drooped like a bandit's, and his vampire-killer's hands looked uncivilized, and his voice rumbled like a tiger in a cellar. The man thought: 'A brigand! A terrorist! I'm going to be kidnapped!'

And he leaped straight in through the revolving doors, so fast they revved behind him like the propeller of a motor boat.

The Bat fluttered in the air in front of Thomas.

'I made a mistake,' it piped. 'Let's try another.'

He flew on down the street and Thomas followed.

3

A woman in a white fox fur flounced out of a hotel. A chauffeur held open the door of a Rolls Royce, and she folded herself inside. Jewels flashed.

Before the door could close, the Bat zinged over the chauffeur's shoulder and followed her in.

Thomas stood helpless. The chauffeur started the car. As it pulled away, Thomas leaped forward.

If this woman was a corrected one, if her mistakes had been wiped clean, if she had started afresh, she could direct him. He saw the Bat on her white fox collar, as he crushed inside and sat beside her. He saw her green eyelids over her round green popping eyes. What she saw was the big, black-moustached, fierce and bristling vampire-killer's face close up against her own.

'A hijacker!' she thought. 'An urban guerrilla! He'll take me off to an attic in Birmingham or Milan. He'll ask for a million pound ransom from my husband.' And she opened her red lips, like an opera singer, to scream.

'Shhhh!' Thomas hissed. 'I want to go back to the beginning. I want to start again. Before we made our mistakes.'

His words were drowned in her scream, loud as a police siren. At the same time, she threw open the opposite door and hurled herself out. Thomas saw lorries and buses going past. His eyes wanted to close in horror but he kept them wide. He saw the woman in the arms of a policeman. And he heard the Bat cry somewhere overhead:

'I've made a mistake!'

Thomas was hauled off to the Police Station.

The police couldn't make head or tail of what Thomas told them. They put him in jail. But he wasn't there long. The Bat came, in its full size, ripped out the barred window, and carried Thomas off to a distant city. They arrived about nine in the evening.

4

'Let's try again,' said the Bat. 'I think I've got it this time. There are two of them together.'

He flew to the front door of a house in a street. Tiny as an ant, he crept in through the keyhole, and undid the lock. Thomas tiptoed in.

A man and his wife sat on a couch in a darkened room watching television. Their faces flickered like bat's wings. They were watching a programme about people on holiday, skiing down bright mountains, surfing on mountainous glittering surf, drinking sparkling drinks beside swimming pools with sharp concrete edges.

The Vampire, now about the same size as Thomas, pointed with a shiny claw to the wife. She was sipping coffee. Her husband was nursing his glass of beer.

'They've got it right,' whispered the Vampire to Thomas. 'They've been corrected, you can see. They've repaired their mistakes. How happy they are! Try her.'

Thomas reached forward, coughed slightly, and tapped the woman on the shoulder. Her face turned. Her mouth opened wide. For a few seconds no sound would come out.

This time Thomas's eyes did close. He knew what had to happen now. Nothing would stop what was coming now.

Sure enough, the scream came. And when it came it went on and on and on. The cat bolted straight into the fireplace, scattering red coals, then changed its mind and shot under the piano. And as the husband jumped up and stared – like a man preparing to leap off a housetop – Thomas, with his eyes still tightly closed, shouted:

'It's all right! It's all right! Calm down! It's all right!'

But then with a bang something hit him and exploded. Everything went black and Thomas sat down.

The television set had come down over his head. By the time he got it off, the happy couple had gone, and the street outside was already full of shouting.

The Bat grabbed Thomas's collar between its fangs.

Outside, the people running from their houses fell back as the great Bat with something in its mouth flew up from the front door, and vanished above the street lights.

5

Next, the Bat flew to the country. Tiny as a bee, it dropped on a farmer's cap, just as he was going out to plough. When the farmer saw Thomas running towards him he thought it was somebody wanting a job. He leaned out of his tractor cab and shouted: 'Not a hope!' then swung his four-bladed plough in through a gateway.

And when Thomas came after him, and shouted over the roar of the tractor: 'I wonder if you can help me. I want to ask you something,' the farmer shouted back: 'Can't talk. Time's money. Ask some other —' and he revved his tractor engine till every rivet was a blur. Then, snuggling his earphones over his ears, and turning up his transistor, he surged away over the field. Thomas stared in frustration at the dark band of glistening furrows and the waving ends of the cut worms.

6

Next, the Bat flew into a painter's studio. The painter looked a little like Thomas. He was big, burly, with a black drooping moustache and big hands blotched with paint. He was painting horizontal pink and blue stripes across his canvas very carefully.

Speaking fast, Thomas explained what he was looking for. The painter kept on painting. He glanced at Thomas now and again. Finally he said, very quietly: 'You sound like a right one!'

Then he grew suddenly angry, and with skilful quick jabs splodged blue paint on Thomas's nose and ears, and told him to clear out, and stop wasting his time, because he'd had enough of madmen to last him a lifetime.

Thomas was a patient man, and because he could at all times feel the vampire-killer inside him, he was always careful to be gentle. But now before he could stop himself he lifted the painter and rolled him like a rolling pin over his tableful of paints, smashing jars and squashing out tubes. And then, with a whole new burst of exasperation, he painted the walls of the room with him, threw him on to his canvas, which collapsed, and stormed out. And when the Bat wailed:

'O where O where is the person we are looking for?'

Thomas shouted: 'He doesn't exist. You're making a fool of me. Look, my wife's mine. I'm going now to get her. You come and change her back to her right size and properly alive, no more games.'

And he grabbed the Bat by its big ears, with his left hand, and pulled out his pistol full of silver bullets with his right hand.

After a moment's silence, the Bat flashed its tongue over its snout and said:

'OK. One more try. If it fails, I promise, she's yours. And I'll go and shut myself up in a Pyramid in Egypt.'

Thomas relaxed his grip. 'One more,' he said. 'Just one more.' And he breathed a deep breath, and closed his eyes for two or three seconds, as if he were saying a short prayer.

7

Thomas and the Vampire Bat sat beside the road, in the edge of a wood. The Vampire was thinking, with little, quick frowns.

Thomas knew what was going on in the Bat's brain. 'Just get it right, this time', he cautioned. 'Otherwise – the Pyramid!'

But the Bat was at its wits' end. It just didn't know where to turn next. All it knew was that the magic person did exist. Time could be made to go backwards. Mistakes could be corrected. It knew that was true.

Suddenly they heard a cry: 'Help!'

The Vampire looked up. Thomas looked at the Vampire.

'Help!' came the faint cry, again.

'It's not far off,' said Thomas, standing up. 'And it's a girl.'

'Funny!' said the Vampire.

'What's funny?' asked Thomas.

They listened.

'Help!' came the cry again.

'It's under the ground,' said the Vampire. 'I heard it in my feet.'

As they stood there listening and puzzling, a grey-haired woman came striding along the road. They watched her, as they listened. She wore dusty leather boots. A faded red dress. A man's old black jacket. She walked slightly bowed, under a ragged rucksack, and of all things she was smoking a pipe. She stopped and looked at them, as they listened and looked at her.

'Show me your hand, big man,' she said. 'And I'll tell you what you can't hear.'

Thomas held out his hand, palm upwards. He was ready for help from anywhere. She stared at the thick palm, still blotched with paint, and the deep red creases, and the powerful trigger-finger.

'This is a blind hand,' she said.

'Don't talk nonsense, my love,' said Thomas. 'All hands are blind. The eyes are in the head.'

'Give me a piece of silver,' she said, 'and I'll open the eyes in this hand.'

Funny sort of gypsy talk, thought Thomas. But he brought out his pistol, ejected one of the silver bullets, and gave it to the tall, grey woman. She stared at him with bright owl's eyes.

The Vampire stared at the silver bullet, now in her hand, with red vampire's eyes. Thomas kept his hand flat out, palm upward, and waited.

Then the woman did a strange thing. She closed her hand over the bullet, and held her closed hand over Thomas's open hand. The Vampire stood very still, watching. As her fingers opened, Thomas expected the silver bullet to drop into his palm.

Instead, a small green snake like a thin necklace untangled from her fingers, and lowered itself on to his palm. It was very cool and silky.

Thomas was so startled he snatched his hand away, and stepped back. The old woman let out a screeching laugh. The Vampire's ears stood up straight. The little snake dropped into the grass and at once began to slide towards the wood.

'Follow it!' she screeched. 'Follow your eyes!' And she pointed after the snake.

Thomas went after it, parting the bracken. He listened for a second, heard it rustle, saw a green gliding pencil of it. He lunged forward, ready to drop on top of it and grab it somehow – and almost fell down a big hole. An old mossy dripping stairway went straight downwards, with bracken and brambles hanging into it. Was it the cellar of a vanished house? He clung there, just managing not to slide head first into it, and saw the snake flowing away down, into the darkness, from step to step.

'Follow it!' came the old woman's yelling laughing voice. 'It's yours! You've paid for it!'

Thomas lowered himself down the stair, after the snake.

Chapter Five
The Kiss Of Truth

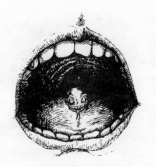

Thomas went down steps into darkness till his thighs ached. At last he saw light below, and coming out under an archway found that he'd stepped from a stumpy ruin of stone tower, that was wrapped with great roots of jungle trees.

Directly ahead of him, from where he stood, a track of flattened, crushed, splintered trees lay open through the jungle. A herd of bulldozers, thought Thomas, have just made the first space for a motorway. This is strange!

He went along that track, stepping from tree to fallen tree, over torn up roots, split, crushed trunks, matted branches. It had only just happened. The leaves still stood fresh. Sap was wet in the gashed bodies of living wood. A red and blue butterfly with a torn wing twitched and fluttered. He picked it up and put it on his head.

As he went, the track became wider.

He heard a child screaming. He found a little black girl, about five years old, trying to clamber up out of the mass of crushed branches. He lifted her out, but she went on screaming, beating his head with her tiny fists.

As he walked along, carrying the screaming child, a black woman came bounding over the fallen trees, snatched the child from him, and set off back to the jungle with her.

'Hey!' shouted Thomas. 'What's happened? What's the matter?'

'The snake!' she yelled back. 'The terrible green snake! It just went through. It flattened the forest. It flattened our village. It might come back!'

She disappeared into the jungle.

The green snake did all this? Well, thought Thomas, it's put on a lot of weight!

The track led to a sheer cliff, and to a split in the cliff. Thomas went into the split, which became a broad-floored tunnel.

He began to find dead bats. Then he saw one creeping up the wall. He picked it off and tried vampire language on it.

'What's happened?' he asked.

The little bat gaped.

'Fright! We've pretty well all died of fright. The snake! Such a snake!'

And he twisted from Thomas's fingers and flew up into the gloom.

Coming out into full light again, Thomas found himself in a street heaped with rubble. He looked back. He'd just come up from an Underground Station. All around, as far as he could see, it was low hills of rubble, with smoke rising here and there, and people stooping and tottering over the heaps. In the distance, skyscrapers shone.

He saw two photographers, in vest and underpants, taking pictures.

'Fantastic!' they were burbling. 'Incredible! Stupendous! Absolutely mind-boggling!'

'What's going on here?' asked Thomas. 'I've just arrived by Underground.'

The men stared at him. Their eyes were rimmed red, their hair was snow-white and stood out all round their heads like the sun's rays.

'A tornado! A green tornado!' cried one. 'It wiped the city flat! What a scoop!'

'I know you'll say we're barmy but it had eyes!' cried the other. 'And it writhed! And it went through here in one hell of a hurry. This was Chicago. Now look!'

'The disaster of the century!' cried the first.

'Of all time,' shouted the other.
'Where's it gone?' shouted Thomas. 'Which way?'

'West!' they called, 'Away west!' and they hurried on, snapping their pictures, as naked people crawled up out of drains, or stumbled in circles carrying television sets, or sat on stones with their heads in their hands.

3

Thomas looked at the smoky sun and turned west, but after only five paces he went straight down an open man-hole.

He fell and he fell. In pitch darkness.

Then he felt a gentle bumping, but he still went on falling.

Then he could see, by a cold blue light like moonlight on snow, that he was sliding down the steep slope of a mountain. Down a long spill of shale, quite gently, slowing as he went.

He got up at the bottom and looked round at a landscape of white volcanoes and lakes of whiteness. He looked up into the sky and thought the round shining globe up there was the moon, till with a shock he recognized the shapes of North and

South America, and there, at the edge, Australia like the head of a Scotch terrier. It was the earth, sailing above him.

So where was he?

Then he noticed dark shapes scurrying over the lakes and slopes. They were all going towards one spot. He set off, tramping across a lake of white dust, climbed over a low hill, and saw in front of him the whole bottom of the valley was missing.

Just a great, more or less round black hole, half a mile across, with sharp edges. And all round the edges, swarms of these dark shapes, hurrying to and fro, crowding to the edges, while more and more of them were coming in from every direction, over the hills and lakes, and passing him at great speed, like skaters racing on ice.

They were people. Or they were like people. But they seemed to be made of cobwebs. They moved among each other with amazing quickness, like the finger of a pianist.

'What's happening?' called Thomas.

Their voices made a familiar noise. Then he remembered. It was like the voice of millions of starlings together. What were they saying? They seemed over-excited. They were so excited they kept breaking away from each other and spinning in a blur, like tops, to burn off the excitement, or leaping in the air and whirling there, like Catherine Wheels, till they dropped back and again peered over the edge into the black drop.

They ignored Thomas. Then he realized – they couldn't hear him. And they didn't seem able to see him either. He strolled about among them trying to catch hold of one. It was no good – their bodies were thin as smoke. They had sharp faces, and their eyes flashed like the dials on a petrol pump. He tried to read whether they were letters or numbers. They were pictures. Their eyes were like tiny televisions playing at tremendous speed.

Then he realized their speech too was tremendously fast. That's why it sounded like squealing millions of birds. He began to catch odd words.

'The snake from heaven.'

'It fell like a spear!'

'It went straight in!' and 'How deep?' and 'Oh, millions of miles deep!'

But as he listened he heard a clear human voice:

'Help!'

He peered down into the crater. And it came again, human and clear, out of the black depth:

'Help!'

A girl's voice.

Thomas looked this way and that. Dare he just leap? That would surely be crazy.

He looked for a sloping crack in the wall of the crater. As he walked along, the milling shadow creatures billowed around him, exactly like smoke.

'Help!' came the voice – from far below.

Thomas stood a while. He'd had some great falls. And here he was, still in one piece. He could see, clearly enough, there was no way down but to leap.

He walked the whole way round the crater, looking for a way down. He wasn't only thinking of the dreadful leap. He was thinking of the way back up, too. Every few minutes, the cry came from the black depths:

'Help!'

After all, he thought, there's more than a voice down there. What about the snake? How big would it be by now? He remembered the tall grey woman's screeching laugh: 'Follow your eyes!'

By now the shadow creatures were piled so high round the crater's edge they looked like the crowded stands at a football stadium. Only they were milling and whirling among themselves, struggling for a better view of the pitch-black hole.

Thomas made up his mind. He stood at the very edge. He breathed a great, deep breath, and he leaped.

And just as he leaped out into the black he heard again, far below:

'Help!'

Then it seemed to him he was in a whirlwind. Instead of falling he was spinning round and round, sinking very gradually in smaller and smaller circles, till at last he was spinning on his backside, on some floor.

He stood up, his legs braced apart, letting the giddiness wear off, and then looked round. Directly in front of him, under a dim lamp, a girl sat in a chair.

4

Thomas gazed at the girl, quite astonished. 'At the bottom of a crater, on some planet,' he was thinking. 'What's she doing here all alone? And where's my snake?'

But the girl only looked at him and cried:

'O thank goodness! Somebody! At last, somebody!'

And covering her face with her hands, she burst into tears.

Thomas comforted her. And it was a long time before she managed to stop sobbing. Then she told him.

'I'm here,' she said, 'in the middle of the moon, because I'm sick. I've a strange sickness. A very strange sickness.'

For a while, she wouldn't tell him what this sickness was. But at last she said:

'Look.'

And she opened her mouth wide, like somebody in a dentist's chair. Thomas angled the lamp, and peered into her mouth.

Over the back of her tongue, under her tonsils, the little green snake peered out at him, with its red-gold eyes.

Then she closed her mouth and burst into tears again.

Thomas simply stood there. He'd tackled vampires of every size and temper. But a green snake, living in a girl's throat! A green snake that had crushed forests and cities.

This is beyond me, he was thinking. I ought to get back to my vampires. But then he remembered his wife, who was lying there as a doll. And the Vampire, her first husband, probably still sitting beside the road, wondering how to find the person who can make time go backward.

But he couldn't help asking the girl: 'How does it feel, having a snake inside?'

She looked at him drearily. She seemed worn out. 'It feels,' she said, 'it feels like – like – '

'Like the Truth!' came the sharp voice from the back of her throat. And again the girl burst into tears, covering her mouth.

What a voice! Even though it had come from her quite small mouth, it sounded to have echoed in a great hall.

'How?' asked Thomas. 'How the Truth? What do you mean, Truth? What is Truth?'

'Show me your finger,' said the snake.

When it spoke, the girl had to open her mouth. She closed her eyes but her mouth opened, and Thomas could see the snake's head inside, peering over the back of her tongue.

He lifted his great, horny, trigger-finger gently. The girl bent forward with her eyes closed, and Thomas thought: she's going to kiss my finger.

Instead, the snake's head flashed out, tapped his knuckles, and flashed back in.

'Hahaha!' laughed the snake. 'Now see. Now you're done for.'

Thomas expected to feel pain beginning, but nothing of the sort happened. He looked at his knuckle to see the fang-marks, and there were two tiny dots. Maybe they'd been there before. Because what he'd felt had seemed just like a kiss.

'What's supposed to happen?' asked Thomas. 'Are you poisonous?'

'I'm the Truth,' cried the snake. 'Now you'll see. You'll change. You'll become what you really are. That's what my deadly bite does to people. It makes them what they really are. You're probably a little fat boy who thinks of nothing but guzzling cakes. Go on. Change.'

But Thomas did not change. The girl was watching him. She seemed to expect him to change too.

'That's funny,' said the snake, in his gloomy hall.

'Usually people do change – completely,' said the girl, still watching Thomas warily. 'They go back to what they really are, to what they were before they started to disguise themselves. You are the first one not to change.'

Thomas was staring at the girl. Her words struck him like a flash of lightning. The old woman with the pipe had been right. She'd opened his eyes.

This was the person – the very person he was looking for. This snake was the one who could make time go backwards. And undo all the mistakes. This snake could sort out the mess.

He grabbed the girl's arm and pulled her to her feet. 'Quick!' he cried.

But then he remembered where he was. He shone the lamp all round. If he was still at the bottom of a hole in the moon, what did it matter if he'd found the magic person – he might be stuck there with her for good.

Then he saw a door. When they stepped out through that door, sunlight was blindingly bright. They stood on a road in a wood.

The Vampire jumped to its feet at the roadside, and came hobbling and flapping towards them. 'Where've you been?' it almost shouted. 'I thought you were a gonner! Is that the girl who cried "Help!"?'

'This,' said Thomas, 'is the girl who can help us.'

5

Thomas gripped the Vampire's neck-fur, the girl rode piggyback on Thomas and inside the girl the snake lay quiet, and so astride the Vampire they flew up and high over the mountains.

When Thomas asked the girl her name, she told him it was Selena. 'It means Moon,' she shouted, against the rushing slipstream of the Bat's flight. 'That's why I love sunbathing. And that's why my hair's jet black.'

Suddenly the Bat dived. Far below, the trees of a mountain forest rose towards them. Thomas saw his tower, at a tilt, in the arms of a giant oak.

The Bat had closed its wings. It fell like a bomb through a hole in the oak's trunk. Thomas braced himself for the crash. The girl gave a little shriek.

But the Bat looped the loop and landed.

They were back in the cellar. And there, just as they'd left her, lay the doll with the shining face, in the chair.

Thomas lost no time.

'Out with you, snake,' he cried. 'Let's have some Truth here. Bite this doll. Prove yourself. Do you hear me, snake?'

Selena picked up the doll. She bent her head and seemed to kiss the doll's brow. Not even Thomas saw the snake's green head flash out and back in again. But he saw the doll's body grow long, till Selena had to let it slide to the floor.

It was his wife! The gorgeous Sweety Crisp! There she was on the floor, on her hands and knees, getting to her feet, looking dazed.

'Oh!' she gasped. 'Oh! I've had a most wonderful dream! The new moon was a boat. I sailed in it. All over heaven. Oh! The most wonderful things I saw! I saw –'

But then she saw Thomas, and the Vampire, and Selena, staring at her, and her face changed as she remembered.

'Whose wife are you?' asked Thomas. His voice was grim. He gazed at her, very solemn. 'We have to get the Truth.'

'You are mine,' said the Vampire.

6

But then Selena put her arms round the Vampire, and the terrible voice of the snake boomed in the low cellar, so that the dangling jewels shivered their lights and tinkled.

'Thomas is Thomas,' said the voice. 'But who are you?'

'No!' cried the Vampire. 'No! Sweety Crisp is my wife! I am the Lord of Vampires.'

'Give him your deadly kiss,' cried Thomas. 'Let's see the Truth.'

And Selena kissed the Vampire's throat.

'Aaaaaaagh!' roared the Vampire, not in pain but in rage because he knew he had lost. He knew what this meant. He knew what the Truth was. His vampire days were over. And the vampire in him bellowed with dismay.

He would kiss no more throats. He would not be snatching Sweety Crisp away from Thomas, to live as his own wife on the vampires' planet. He tore himself free from Selena's arms. He sank on to the chair where the doll had lain, clutching his throat and moaning, as the bite of Truth worked on him.

And he changed.

In front of their eyes he became an old man. He sat for a while, looking at the floor, and clasping and unclasping his long bony fingers. Then he stood up, tall. He wore a long white robe of woolly rough cloth. His face, no longer anything like a vampire, was more like an old eagle's, thin and sharp, and his great eagle eyes looked at them each in turn. It was the face of a fierce, old man.

'Now,' he said at last, 'there is hope for me.'

And without another word he left them. He climbed the spiral stair, out of the oak tree, and went on away up into the mountains, looking for his cave. And there he became the Holy Man of the mountains, talking to eagles.

7

Thomas and Sweety looked at Selena, and she looked at them. What a weird power the little snake had!

Thomas wanted to ask her who she was, and where she had come from. And what was the story of the snake? There was much he wanted to ask about the snake.

But at that moment the stair rattled, and they all looked up, alarmed. Was the Holy Man coming back? Had the Truth worn off already? Had he turned back into the Lord of Vampires, and was he returning to reclaim Sweety Crisp? Thomas put his left arm round Sweety, and his right hand closed round the hilt of his pistol.

A dark furry figure came limping down, dragging a black cloak of wings. Claws clashed on the wooden steps.

'It's Ffangs!' Sweety Crisp almost screamed with delight. 'Oh, poor little Ffangs!'

'I've been travelling for three nights,' croaked Ffangs. 'How good it is to see my friends. I knew I'd find you.'

'What's happened?' asked Thomas. 'How's trade at the Beefeater's Bistro?'

They heard his tale.

He was sick of the restaurant. He was sick of customers and of their hands endlessly stuffing food into their gnashing faces. He was sick of strawberries and cream.

'If I see one more dollop of cream,' he said,' I'll jump into a cauldron of boiling silver.'

'A kiss!' cried Selena. 'I can see he needs a kiss.'

And she put her arms round his neck and kissed the furry corner of his mouth, near the fangs.

It was a shock for all of them. Even Selena, who had just kissed her second vampire bat, jumped backwards.

Where Ffangs had stood, with his crooked vampire feet, and his trailing wings, and his unhappy little red eyes, was a bright lad.

He had gold hair, sprinkled with glittering lights, and a bright face, as if he had just come from a hot bath, and he was dressed as the joker in the card pack. He was so bright, it seemed he might leap over them all. He stared at his hands, astonished. He held them up, and curled his strange new fingers – but they would not be claws, they stayed fingers.

'I've made it!' he yelled. 'I'm human!'

They, too, stared at him astonished. Who would have thought? He was overjoyed. But then his face changed. Suddenly he looked anxious. His hand moved to his pocket. As if he had dreamed it, and were now finding it real, he brought out a letter. He opened it. And his face changed even more as he read it.

'Well?' said Thomas, 'What news?'

The Bright Lad looked up. He had the strangest little baffled frown on his face.

'Who am I?' he asked.

They stared. Who was he? He had been Ffangs the vampire bat. But now – yes, who was he?

Couldn't he remember?

'It says here,' the Bright Lad read: 'Selena is your sister. She'll tell you who you are.'

Selena screamed out – but clapped her hands over her mouth. They stared at each other – the black-haired girl and the Bright Lad.

But before they could say one more word, even before Selena could take the hands from her mouth, the room shook.

'Here it comes again!' thought Thomas, and he gripped Sweety Crisp tighter in his left arm, while his right hand grabbed the bottom post of the staircase. But then the floor itself leaped, and tossed them all in the air.

A bang like a striking thunderbolt deafened them. And the room split. As if the oak tree had been split from top to bottom by a thunderbolt. And indeed there did come a blinding flash with it.

Thomas just managed to glimpse a gigantic red hand – a skinny, wide-spreading, red hand – plunge in through the flash and snatch up Selena.

As the red spots cleared from their eyes, Thomas and Sweety Crisp got up off the floor. Sunlight streamed in through the split wall. Gems from the festoons of dangling glitter covered the floor, like fresh hailstones. Small puffs of white cloud sat about in the blue sky. Birds sang in the oak trees all round. But Selena, with the snake inside her, had vanished.

Then Thomas saw the Bright Lad out in the sunlight, running to and fro, among the oak trees, in his joker colours. Thomas thought he might have been knocked crazy by the flash and bang.

'Are you all right?' he called.

The Bright Lad stopped and stared. He didn't look all right at all. His eyes were round and wild.

'I've got to find her,' he suddenly shouted, and began to run away through the trees.

'Come back,' bellowed Thomas. 'You'll need help.'

'I've got to find her,' came the voice. 'I've got to find her.' And fainter and fainter, from deeper and deeper in the forest, it came: 'I've got to find her.'

Thomas gazed after the voice. Sweety Crisp watched his face. She could see his thoughts racing. She was expecting him to leap away after the Bright Lad, and leave her all on her own again.

She noticed a butterfly trying to free itself from the rough, black hair on top of Thomas' head. It flexed its red and blue wings, took off, and flew dithering up into the sunlight, and away over the dazzling leaves of the oak trees, as if it were following the voice.

Thomas frowned and turned to look at Sweety Crisp. But all he said was: 'He's going to need help.'

(*The adventures of Ffangs will be continued in the next book.*)